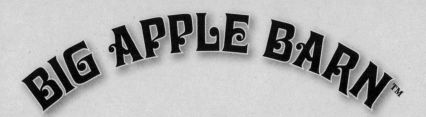

HAPPY'S BIG PLAN

WELCOME TO
BIG APPLE BARN!

HAPPY'S BIG PLAN

by **KRISTIN EARHART**

Illustrations by
JOHN STEVEN GURNEY

A
LITTLE APPLE
PAPERBACK

SCHOLASTIC INC.
New York Toronto London Auckland Sydney
Mexico City New Delhi Hong Kong Buenos Aires

To Brant and Wilson, who know what it takes to make a good team.

With love, K.J.E.

ISBN-13: 978-0-439-90094-2
ISBN-10: 0-439-90094-8

12 11 10 9 8 7 6 5 4 3 2   7 8 9 10 11/0
                                          40

Printed in the U.S.A.
First printing, November 2006

Contents

Chapter One

The Big Day

Happy Go Lucky bit off a mouthful of clover and looked around the field. He was grazing next to his friends, Goldilocks and Big Ben, but there were lots of other ponies and horses in the pasture. Happy had lived at Big Apple Barn for only a few weeks. He was finally starting to feel at home. And just in time. Today he would become a true school pony.

Happy took a whiff of the fresh afternoon air. He smelled something familiar. *I hope it*

doesn't rain, Happy thought. He looked up into the sky. It was a deep blue, and the clouds looked as light and fluffy as white dandelions. It didn't look like bad weather, yet Happy knew that smell meant rain. And he didn't want his first lesson to be in the rain.

"What are you thinking about, Happy?" Goldi asked, nudging him with her muzzle.

Happy liked Goldi. She was a small, caramel-colored pony with a blond mane and tail. Goldi was much older than Happy, and she had a lot more experience as a school pony. In fact, she had been friends with Happy's mother a long time ago. They had learned how to be school ponies together. Even though Happy trusted Goldi, he wasn't sure he wanted to tell her what was on his mind — especially with Big Ben there. Big Ben was the top horse in the barn. How could he understand?

"Are you worried about your first lesson?" Goldi wondered. She could tell what was wrong, even though Happy hadn't said anything. "You shouldn't be. You'll be a great school pony."

Happy was glad she thought so, but how could she know? Happy was still young. Only two people had ever ridden him. The first person was Mrs. Shoemaker. How Happy loved her! Mrs. Shoemaker had trained him when he lived at Shoemaker Stables with his mom. Mrs. Shoemaker had taught Happy how to carry a rider and listen to the rider's commands.

Then, three weeks ago, a woman named Diane came to Shoemaker Stables to look at Happy. Diane bought him from Mrs. Shoemaker and brought him to Big Apple Barn. There, Happy carried his second rider ever. Her name was Andrea, and she was Diane's older daughter. Andrea was a good rider, but it still took a while for Happy to get used to working with her.

It took him a while to get used to his new home, too. Big Apple Barn was big, and there were a lot more horses and ponies there than he had ever seen before. Happy had heard Diane say that she had about twenty horses and ten ponies, and almost all of them were part of the riding school. Today, Happy would officially become part of the school, too.

Happy looked from Goldi to Big Ben and took a deep breath. "I *am* worried," he said. "What if I don't know what to do? What if I can't tell what my rider wants in my lesson?"

To Happy's relief, Big Ben kept eating. Goldi paused, then gave Happy a knowing look. "It can be hard to understand a new rider at first," she admitted. "But you have to pay close attention to what your rider asks."

Happy nodded, listening to what his friend had to say.

"There's one thing you should know," Goldi advised. "You'll be given better riders at first. You're new, so Diane will make sure your riders know as much as or more than you do."

Happy wasn't sure how he felt about that. What if the rider knew *too* much and asked Happy to do things he wasn't ready to do?

"And remember," Goldi continued in a soothing tone. "Diane will be there to make sure the rider does a good job."

Diane was in charge of the riding school.

People came to Big Apple Barn to learn how to ride horses and ponies. Happy would help them learn. If the rider knew how to ask him to do something, then he would do it. But if they didn't ask him the right way, then he would not be able do what they wanted him to do.

Happy shook his head. What a huge responsibility. And a scary one, too. A brand-new person would ride him that day, and lots of new people would ride him in the weeks to come. Happy let out a sigh. Just thinking about it made him dizzy.

"I know how you feel, kid."

Happy blinked in surprise when he heard the low, noble voice. It was Big Ben. The tall chestnut horse was looking right at him.

"It isn't always easy," Big Ben confided. "But it's worth it. Sometimes you'll get a

rider who really understands you, and that's one of the best feelings in the world."

Big Ben had a soft look in his eyes. He stood there for a moment before lowering his head for another bite of clover.

Happy thought about the horse's words. He wanted to find a rider like that — someone who could understand him.

Just then, Happy heard his name.

"Happy!" Diane called. The trainer was standing by the pasture gate, her long hair blowing in the breeze. In one hand, she held a lead rope. That could only mean one thing. It was almost time for Happy's first lesson as a school pony. Happy knew he had a lot to learn, but he hoped he had something to teach a rider, too.

"Good luck, Happy," Goldilocks said.

"Give it your best," Big Ben added.

"Thanks," Happy answered. Then he turned toward the gate and picked up a trot. He was excited. He had a job to do.

Diane gave Happy a pat and hooked the lead rope to his halter. He walked next to her. Happy was so busy thinking about the lesson ahead that he didn't notice the dark clouds gathering in the sky.

Chapter Two

The New Rider

Diane led Happy into his stall and closed the door behind him. "Rest up, Happy," Diane said. "Emily will be here soon for her lesson."

Happy tossed his head to tell Diane that he understood. Diane smiled and walked away.

"Oh, I'm glad you're back," a small voice squeaked from the floor of the stall.

Happy turned around, searching for the

voice's owner. Finally he spotted Roscoe, the barn mouse, who was rummaging for loose kernels of corn on the ground. Roscoe scurried over to a mound of grain in the corner and emptied the heap in his front legs onto the pile. As he brushed the dust off his paws, he looked up at Happy.

"We have a lot to talk about and not much time," Roscoe said.

Happy remembered that Diane had said he should rest up, but he knew he wouldn't be able to do that with Roscoe around.

"Hello, Roscoe," Happy greeted the mouse. "What do we need to talk about?"

Roscoe shook his head. "Your lesson, of course," he said. "Did you forget?"

"Um, no," Happy assured his friend. "I've been thinking about it all day."

"Good, so have I," Roscoe said. "You heard Diane. Emily will ride you this afternoon. Emily's been coming here a long time. She used to ride Romeo."

Happy listened closely.

"Romeo wasn't the best school pony. He didn't listen very well," Roscoe said. Then he sighed. "Well, to be honest, he just wasn't very smart. But he was handsome, and lots of lesson riders liked him."

Happy wasn't sure why Roscoe was telling him this. What did it have to do with *his* lesson?

"So, Emily had her lessons on Romeo for at least a year. He was her favorite. Then another one of Romeo's riders bought him from Diane. That was a couple of weeks ago. You're the first pony that Emily's ridden since then," Roscoe finished.

"Okay," Happy said uncertainly. "I'll keep that in mind." But Happy didn't think it would change anything. He would do his best, and he would hope that Emily liked him.

"Good," Roscoe replied. "I'm glad I got the chance to tell you. Now I need to get back home. I'll check on you later." Roscoe gave Happy's hoof a pat. Then he headed back to the grain pile in the corner and gathered up as many kernels as he could carry.

Happy put his head over the stall door to watch Roscoe walk toward the hay barn, which was where he slept at night. The pony laughed to himself as the mouse left a golden trail of corn nuggets behind him.

Then he saw Diane walking toward him. A dark-haired girl followed two steps behind her. The girl

looked like she was close to Andrea's age, and she had warm, thoughtful eyes.

"Emily, I'd like you to meet Happy," Diane said. "He's new here. He has a lovely long stride. You're ready to ride a pony with more energy. I think you and Happy will have a lot of fun together."

Happy pricked his ears forward and tried to look like a lot of fun.

"You can use the same saddle you used on Romeo," Diane continued. "And Happy's bridle is in the tack room. It hangs right under his name." Diane paused and looked at the young rider. "I'll leave you to brush him. See you in the ring outside."

"Thanks," Emily said. She opened Happy's stall door and grasped his halter. "Come on, Happy," she said. She led him down the aisle to the cross ties. She did not say a word

as she picked his hooves and combed his mane.

"I have to get the saddle," she announced before she turned and walked away.

Happy thought Emily seemed nice, but very quiet.

Then Happy saw somebody at the end of the barn aisle.

It was Ivy! Ivy was Diane's younger daughter. Happy liked her. Ivy knew just where to scratch a pony behind his ears. Plus, she gave Happy treats from time to time. When Happy was brand new at Big Apple Barn, Ivy had offered him a gigantic, delicious apple. It had helped Happy feel at home.

Happy was glad to see Ivy. He had been looking out for her lately, but she had not been to visit him for a while. Now she was there, just at the other end of the row of stalls. She was busy petting an orange barn cat. But Happy wasn't too concerned with the cat. He wanted to get Ivy's attention. He whinnied a hello.

Ivy's braids bounced a little as she looked up. Happy thought he saw her smile.

"I'm back," Emily said softly. Happy

15

turned to look at his new rider. She had a saddle and his bridle. So, this was it — his first lesson at Big Apple Barn.

Happy wondered if Ivy had come to the barn to watch his first lesson. He hoped so. It would be comforting to have her there. But when Happy looked back down the aisle for his friend, Ivy was gone.

Chapter Three

A First Lesson

Emily led Happy toward the big barn doors. Happy hoped he would see Ivy outside, but only Diane was in the outdoor ring.

"Great, Emily," Diane called. "How about you walk Happy to the stair block, so you can get on," Diane said.

Emily clicked her tongue and pulled lightly on the reins. Happy followed. As he did, he noticed a light wind. He looked up and shivered. Dark clouds hovered in the sky. Happy was sure it would rain.

Emily stopped Happy by the stair block and climbed up the wooden steps, so she could reach the stirrup. Happy stood still while Emily pulled herself into the saddle.

"You look good on him, Emily," Diane said. "How about you tell Happy to walk around the ring and get used to his stride."

"Okay," Emily said, giving Happy a squeeze with her legs.

Happy knew this was his chance to get used to Emily, too. She held the reins kind of tight, so Happy guessed she might be a little scared. *It's only fair,* he thought. *She doesn't know what kind of pony I might be.* Happy wanted to prove to her that he was a good pony.

Diane called for them to trot. Emily gave Happy a light kick, and he sprang forward.

Happy lifted his legs high and arched his neck with each step. He listened closely to Emily. He thought his first lesson was going well, but then he felt a brisk breeze. He tried to ignore the wind as it whirled around him, tugging at his mane and tail. Happy shook his neck, pulling the reins through Emily's hands.

"Oh!" Emily exclaimed.

"That's okay, Emily," Diane reassured her student. "Just shorten the reins and ask Happy to keep trotting."

Emily did as Diane said. But Happy could still feel the wind. He had to squint to see, and it was hard to concentrate.

Happy was anxious that it might rain any minute, but he knew he needed to listen to Emily. They trotted around the ring in both directions. Then they walked.

"Ask him to canter when you're ready," Diane told Emily.

Happy waited for Emily to give him the signs. Happy decided not to worry about the weather because he was excited to canter. The canter was his favorite gait. It was much faster than a trot. Fun! It took a while for Emily to tell Happy what to do. Emily was not as quick as Mrs. Shoemaker had been. Emily took her time. After she pulled on the inside rein, she waited a moment. Then, all at once, she gave Happy a big kick in the side.

Oh! Happy gasped. The kick surprised him. He bolted forward into a canter. He made quick, short steps.

"Whoa!" Emily gasped.

"That's okay," Diane reassured her as she watched. "Happy listens well. He doesn't need you to ask as hard as some ponies, like Romeo. But you're doing fine."

Happy gulped. Were they really doing fine? He wasn't so sure. They *were* cantering, but it didn't feel like when Mrs. Shoemaker cantered him. Emily bounced around in the saddle. She slapped up and down on his back. It didn't feel good.

"He feels so bumpy!" Emily exclaimed. She sounded upset. Happy didn't know what to do.

"Emily, put your heels down and sit back," Diane called. "Hold on with your legs, and then he won't seem as bumpy."

Emily did what Diane said, and Happy could tell she wasn't hitting his back as hard. Happy relaxed a little, and he evened out his stride.

"Better?" Diane asked.

"Yeah," Emily said. Happy agreed. It felt better to him, too.

Emily was a strong, young rider, but she was still learning. Happy now knew what that meant. When a rider was still learning, it might take her longer to tell a pony just what to do. She might not know all the right signs, or she might hold the reins too tight. Or she might not be able to sit in the saddle so it felt nice and smooth.

Emily cantered Happy around the ring a couple of times. Then Diane told Emily to turn around and canter in the other direction. This time, Emily asked Happy to canter right away. *And* she sat back in the saddle.

Happy breathed a sigh of relief when Diane told Emily to walk. The lesson was over. Happy had worried over nothing. It hadn't rained, and Emily had been nice. Happy didn't think it was as nice as having Mrs. Shoemaker on his back, but he still felt good.

Soon, Emily had put Happy back in his stall. "So, how do you like our new pony?" Diane asked.

"He was good, I guess," Emily said. "But I miss Romeo."

Diane raised her eyebrows. "Oh, I know how you feel," she replied. "It is hard when your favorite pony leaves. But I think you and Happy are good together. You can teach each other a lot."

Emily nodded.

Diane smiled and walked away.

Emily patted Happy's nose and fed him a carrot. "Thanks, Happy," she said. Then she turned and left the barn.

Happy ate the carrot, but he forgot to think about how sweet and tasty it was. He was busy thinking about his first lesson. It went well, he decided. But it wasn't like what Big Ben had talked about. It wasn't like he and Emily had really understood each other. Happy guessed he would have to wait a while to find a rider like that.

Chapter Four

Ivy and Prudence

The next day, Happy was busy watching all of the activity in the barn. He had his head over the stall door. Out of the corner of his eye, Happy spotted a young girl at the other end of the barn. It was Ivy, and she was with that orange tabby cat again!

Happy wanted to whinny to her, but then he remembered what had happened the day before. He had whinnied to Ivy then, and she had disappeared without saying hello. He missed Ivy, and he wondered why she wouldn't come to visit him. Had he done something wrong?

Suddenly, a voice cut into his thoughts. "Whatcha thinking?"

Happy jumped a little. "Roscoe!" he exclaimed. "I thought I told you not to sneak up on me like that."

"Like what?" Roscoe asked. He had crawled up the wood planks of the stall so he could sit on the door, right next to Happy's head. "Really, I'm a mouse. What else can I do?"

Happy had to admit, his friend had a point. "Maybe next time, you should say my name first, so you don't surprise me as much."

"Okay then," Roscoe agreed, nodding. "Hello, Happy. Whatcha thinking?"

Happy sighed. "I was thinking about Ivy. She's been hanging out at the far end of the barn lately. With that scruffy old cat."

"Oh," Roscoe said. "Well, today is Ivy's lesson day. And that scruffy old cat is Prudence."

So that's *Prudence*, Happy thought. Roscoe had told him a lot about Prudence. She had been the barn cat for a long time, and she had predicted that Happy and Goldilocks would be friends. Prudence had been right about that. Goldi was a good friend.

"Ivy and Prudence are real chums," Roscoe said.

"Oh, that's good," Happy said. "So Ivy has a lesson today? Who does Ivy ride?" Happy tried to sound like he was just making chitchat, but he was very curious.

"Well, she's still a beginner. And all of the beginners ride Goldi," Roscoe said, wandering over to Happy's water bucket.

"Really?" Happy was surprised.

"Yeah. Goldi's good with them," Roscoe said. "Ivy just started jumping, and Goldi takes things nice and slow." He looked in the bucket at his reflection. He cleaned off his mouth and whiskers with his paws. "Why?" Roscoe asked.

But Happy didn't get a chance to answer because just then Diane walked into the barn. Many of the horses nickered when they saw her. Happy and Roscoe turned to watch.

"Hello, honey," Diane said to Ivy. "Have you brushed Goldi yet?"

"Um, not yet," Ivy responded. "I wanted to ask you something first."

Ivy and Diane were still at the other end of the barn, so Happy could barely hear them.

"Could I . . ." Ivy began. "Is there any way . . ." Ivy tried again, but she stopped. Ivy took a deep breath and looked up at her mother. "Can I ride Happy in my lesson today?" she asked.

Happy's heart raced. Ivy wanted to ride him! He held his breath. Roscoe walked along the stall door toward Happy and placed a reassuring paw on the pony's nose.

"Absolutely not," Diane responded. Her words did not sound mean, but her tone was firm.

Ivy made a short sniffing sound.

"Happy is still very young. He has a lot to learn about being a school pony," Diane explained. "And you are too new to riding to teach him."

"But Emily hasn't been riding much longer than me," Ivy argued.

"That's true," Diane said. "But Emily is bigger. If something went wrong, she would be able to handle Happy. You aren't that strong yet."

Ivy opened her mouth, but then she closed it with a sigh.

Happy did the same. What Diane had said didn't make sense to him. He wanted Ivy to ride him, and Ivy wanted the same. It didn't seem fair. What could go wrong?

"Go ahead and get Goldi ready," Diane said.

It wasn't long before Happy and Roscoe heard the light *clip-clop* of Goldi, the short, pretty pony, coming down the aisle. Ivy was petting her long, blond mane as they walked. When Ivy got close to Happy's stall, she looked over.

Happy tossed his head to say hello.

Ivy gave him a shy, sad smile, and then glanced away.

Happy stamped his foot. He wanted Ivy to look back at him. He wanted her to know he thought she should ride him, too, but Ivy kept walking.

The pony and mouse watched as Ivy and Goldi headed toward the outdoor arena.

"You want her to ride you, don't you?" Roscoe asked.

"Yeah," Happy said, scuffing his hoof on the ground.

"I'm sorry," Roscoe said.

"I'm sorry, too," Happy replied.

Just then, Prudence padded up the aisle. She watched until Ivy and Goldi were out of sight. Then she turned to Happy. She raised her head and stared at the young pony with her deep green eyes. She looked Happy up and down. With a huff, the cat sat back on her hind legs and began to clean her front paws. "I'm not sorry at all," she said.

Chapter Five

Ivy and Goldi

Happy couldn't believe how rude Prudence was! He was upset, and she didn't care in the least. Not only that, but the cat was still sitting right in front of his stall. She had cleaned herself from head to toe — twice — yet she stayed put.

Roscoe had tried to give Happy and Prudence a proper introduction, but Prudence would not listen. She had simply announced that she wasn't sorry that Ivy couldn't ride Happy, and she hadn't uttered a word since.

Rude, rude, rude.

Finally, Happy had stepped back into his stall. He didn't like the way Prudence looked at him, and he didn't want her to hear everything he and Roscoe were saying. They needed some privacy.

Happy was glad that Ivy wanted to ride him. Now he understood why she had been acting so shy. She wasn't trying to stay away from him. She was just disappointed.

Happy was disappointed, too.

"I thought Diane liked me," Happy said to Roscoe.

"Of course she does," Roscoe answered.

"It's not that she doesn't like you. She just doesn't think Ivy is ready to ride you yet."

Happy understood what Roscoe was saying, but it wasn't what he wanted to hear.

"Goldi has been the beginners' pony for a long time. She doesn't do any of the bad "B" things," Roscoe said.

"The bad "B" things?" Happy questioned. "What are you saying?"

"I'm saying this," Roscoe explained. "She doesn't buck. She doesn't bolt. She doesn't bite." He counted each "B" on his fingers. "Those are three things a beginners' pony should not do."

"I don't do any of those things!" Happy said.

"Of course you don't," Roscoe agreed. "At least not when you can help it. But I've heard Diane explain the bad "B" things before.

Sometimes we get nervous or scared, and we do things we normally would not do. Not just ponies — even mice like myself. And people, too. You never know," Roscoe said with a shrug. "But Goldi doesn't get nervous much. She's been around a while, and Diane can trust her."

Happy listened to what Roscoe had to say. It made sense.

His ears perked up when he heard hooves on the aisle floor.

"It's Goldi," Roscoe announced, standing on his tiptoes so he could see down the aisle. "She looks wet. It must be raining. I guess she and Ivy will have to finish their lesson inside."

"Come on," Happy said. "Let's watch!"

Roscoe jumped onto his friend's nose and scurried up toward his ears. There, the mouse sat down and held on to the long silky hairs of Happy's mane.

Happy turned to the back of his stall and lowered his head. There was a gap in the wall, and it was just the right size for seeing what was going on in the indoor ring. Happy had never had a lesson in the indoor ring, and he was curious to see how it was different.

As Happy watched, he could tell that Goldi was a good riding pony. She didn't yank the reins out of the rider's hands. She didn't go too fast. She was smooth and steady all the way. Happy thought Goldi might be *too* good. When Diane said, "Stop," Goldi stopped. Goldi didn't even wait for Ivy to pull on the reins.

"I don't want to cause any problems," Roscoe said. "But Ivy looks kind of bored."

Happy agreed, but he didn't want to say so — especially not with Prudence sitting right outside his stall. What if the cat told Goldi what he said?

"And Goldi looks bored, too," Roscoe added. It was true. There was no bounce in Goldi's step. She was being good, but she didn't seem to be having fun.

"Maybe there is some way for Ivy to ride

you after all," Roscoe said. "We could come up with a plan to change Diane's mind." The mouse rubbed his paws together. "You know who could help?" he asked.

"Who?" Happy replied.

"Prudence."

Happy wasn't so sure that was a good idea. Roscoe raised his eyebrows and pointed to the front of the stall. "She's very wise. She knows a lot about this place — and about Diane."

Happy had to agree with that. He turned around in his stall and walked to the front. He braced himself for facing the tough tabby cat again. But when he and Roscoe looked over the door and into the barn aisle, Prudence wasn't there.

Chapter Six

Andrea's Advice

The next day, Happy heard Ivy's voice in the barn. He rushed to look over his stall door. When Happy glanced down the aisle, he saw that Ivy was not alone. Her mom and her sister, Andrea, were with her. Andrea was older than Ivy, and she had ridden horses a lot longer.

As Happy watched, he realized Diane and her daughters were coming to see him.

Happy wondered what they were saying. He pricked his ears forward.

"I agree with Mom," Andrea said.

"But Andrea," Ivy complained. Her eyes were big, and she was holding her hands together.

"Ivy, wait until you hear what your sister has to say," Diane advised. "After all, she knows Happy well."

Happy listened closely. He, of course, knew Andrea well, too. Andrea had been the first person to ride him at Big Apple Barn, and she had ridden him many times in the past three weeks. But it was the first ride that Happy really remembered. He had been anxious and had a lot of energy. He had run very fast, even though Andrea had only asked him to trot. Happy had a bad feeling Andrea remembered that, too.

"Happy's a good pony," Andrea said. "He really improved after that first ride."

Happy grumbled to himself. He knew she'd bring that up!

"But he's still green," Andrea added.

"What?" Ivy asked. "Happy is brown, not green!" She reached out and tickled Happy's soft nose.

"Ivy," Andrea said in a big-sister tone, "if you knew more about horses, you would understand. Green doesn't mean that he's green in color. It means that he is still early in his training. He doesn't have a lot of experience."

"Oh," Ivy said.

"I told her the same thing," Diane said in a motherly tone. "Ivy, you're just not ready for him yet, and he's not ready for you. Be patient, dear." Diane put a hand on Ivy's shoulder and gave it a squeeze. "I'm going

to tack Big Ben up now," she said. "See you two soon."

When Diane had left, Ivy turned to her sister. "Why didn't you stick up for me? You're such a good rider, you can ride any horse you want. I just want to ride Happy."

"I understand, Ivy," Andrea said in a soft voice. "Really, I do." Andrea reached out and tightened Ivy's ponytails so the rubber bands didn't fall out. Then she patted Ivy on the head.

Ivy cringed. "If you understand, then why didn't you help me convince Mom?"

"Here's the deal," Andrea said. "Mom wouldn't have listened to me. She needs proof. She needs to see that you and Happy have a special bond. Then she'll let you ride him."

"Really?" Ivy's voice was full of hope.

"It might take a while, but she'll come around," Andrea said. "You're too young to remember how I got her to let me ride Gracie. I was just about your age."

Happy had been listening closely, but now he was really interested. Gracie was Happy's mom. Before Gracie lived at Shoemaker Stables, she had been a school pony at Big Apple Barn. And now Happy knew that Andrea had ridden her! Happy wondered if his mom had wanted Andrea to ride her as much as he wanted Ivy to ride him.

"It'll work out," Andrea said. She gave her sister a smile. Then she left Ivy and Happy alone.

Ivy let herself into Happy's stall. "Hello, boy," she whispered. "I have something for you." Ivy held out a carrot stump.

Happy smelled it right away. With his lips, he lifted the carrot off Ivy's hand. Then he licked her fingers to make sure he didn't miss anything. Ivy giggled.

"You are very special, Happy," Ivy said. "You're my favorite pony." She paused. She started to scratch Happy behind the ears. He loved that. "I don't care if you are green," she told him. "I trust you. And I will figure out a way to show Mom that we are good together. I promise. I think we could be a great team."

Happy put his head over Ivy's shoulder and nuzzled her back. He was glad to hear her say all of that. He agreed.

Chapter Seven

The Secret Plan

A few days went by, and Happy had a few more lessons. Each time, he worked with a different rider. And each time, Diane told him he did a good job. Like Emily, Happy's other riders were all older and taller than Ivy. They were all nice, too. Happy enjoyed being a school pony, but one thing didn't seem quite right. He still didn't understand why Ivy couldn't ride him in her lessons.

When Happy wasn't having a lesson, he usually stayed in his stall. On nice days, he was sometimes turned out in the grassy field. But it had been raining a lot lately, so he had spent extra time inside. Thank goodness for Roscoe! The young mouse came to see Happy every day.

Roscoe made Happy laugh, but he wasn't just a jokester. He was also very clever. When it came to important things, Roscoe was all business. At those times, the mouse would tug on his ear and scratch his chin and think and think and think.

Roscoe had not forgotten what Ivy had said to her mother. He knew Ivy wanted to ride Happy. And on one very drizzly day, Roscoe helped Happy come up with a plan to make sure that Ivy could ride Happy soon. It was such a good plan, Roscoe said they didn't even need to ask Prudence for help.

Neither Roscoe nor Happy had talked to Prudence in more than a week. The tabby cat always seemed to show up when Ivy was in the barn. When Ivy was around, Prudence would purr and rub against the girl's legs. She'd speak in soft meows to get Ivy's attention. But it was another story when Ivy was away. Prudence would prowl through the stable, her eyes aglow and her tail twitching. She would sometimes sit across from Happy's stall and watch him without saying a single word.

"Our plan is foolproof," Roscoe said to Happy in the stall one day. "It is the only way to prove that you and Ivy belong together."

"Okay, okay," Happy said, but he wasn't so sure. One thing he did know was that he missed Ivy. She still came by Happy's stall, but she always had a sad smile on her face. Happy wanted her to give him a real smile again. "Okay," Happy agreed. "I'll do it. For Ivy."

"For Ivy," Roscoe said.

A few days later, Happy got his chance to put the plan into action. He was out in the field with Goldi, Ben, and some other horses. Since the weather had been stormy, it had been several days since Happy had gone out to the pasture. He needed to stretch his legs! Happy cantered around the field again and again. He only stopped briefly to say hello to his friends, tell them about his lessons, and take a bite or two of clover.

When Diane and Andrea showed up at the gate to bring in the horses, Happy wasn't ready. He still wanted to run, and he still wanted more clover.

"See you soon, Happy," Goldi called as she walked toward Andrea.

"Glad your lessons are going well," Ben said as Diane clipped the lead rope to his halter.

"Thank you," Happy replied. "See you soon!" He was glad his friends were going back into the barn. He didn't want them to see what he was about to do.

He watched the other horses and ponies head for the gate, one by one. Everything

was going according to plan. Finally, Happy was the last pony in the field.

"Happy," Andrea yelled. "It's time to come in." Diane's older daughter stood by the pasture gate, shaking a lead rope.

Happy looked at her and dropped his head down to eat some grass.

"Happy!" Andrea yelled again.

Happy pretended he didn't hear her. Then another voice joined Andrea's.

"Come on, Happy," Diane called.

Happy raised his head. He wanted to go to Diane, but he knew it wasn't part of the plan. This was tough!

Happy watched. Diane said something to Andrea. Then she opened the gate and walked into the field.

"Here, Happy," Diane said. She walked toward the pony, holding her hand out. Happy reached down to nip off another clump of grass. When Diane was just a couple of steps from him, Happy lifted his head and trotted away.

"Now, Happy," Diane called. "What are you doing? You're always so good about coming in from the field."

Happy swished his tail and kept trotting. He didn't stop until he reached the clover patch. Then he dropped his head again. Happy looked to see how close Diane was. As he glanced around, something in the distance caught his eye.

Prudence. The barn cat was sitting on top of one of the fence posts, and she was watching Happy. *Oh, great,* Happy thought. *That's just what I need. Now she* really *won't like me.*

"It's okay, Happy," Diane said softly. "Let's go inside so you can get some dinner." Happy thought that dinner sounded good, but it was not part of the plan. Just as Diane reached out to grab his halter, Happy dashed away.

"Happy," Diane said. This time her voice was louder, and Happy could tell she was not pleased. Andrea joined her mom, and they watched Happy as he nibbled on a flower of clover. They whispered to each other. Happy flicked his ear to the side, trying to hear what they said.

Then he heard just what he'd been waiting for. "Hey! What are you guys doing?" a voice called. Happy looked around. There she was — Ivy! She was standing by the fence, petting Prudence.

"Happy won't come in," Diane called across the field.

"He won't let us catch him," Andrea explained.

"But that's not like Happy," Ivy said.

"I know," Diane said.

Happy kept eating, but he was paying close attention. Ivy gave Prudence a last pet and climbed over the fence. She headed toward her mother and sister at first.

But then Ivy turned toward Happy. She walked right up to him.

"Hello, boy," Ivy said. "What are you up to?"

Happy nickered a hello and raised his head.

"Would you like to go back to your stall now?" she asked.

Happy tossed his head up and down.

"Okay then, let's go," Ivy said. She scratched behind his ear and then took hold of his halter.

Without another word, Ivy and Happy headed to the barn.

When they passed Andrea and Diane, Happy saw Ivy's big sister give her a thumbs-up. Diane simply shook her head as her younger daughter walked by with the brown pony right at her side.

As they passed Prudence, Happy was certain he saw her roll her eyes. But Happy didn't care what the tabby cat was thinking.

The plan had worked!

Chapter Eight

Good News

Ivy ran into the barn the next day. She was out of breath by the time she got to Happy's stall.

"Oh, Happy! I have so much to tell you," Ivy exclaimed. "Mom couldn't believe that you followed me into the barn yesterday. She says we must have a special understanding," Ivy explained. She smiled and petted his velvety nose.

Happy let out a sigh of relief. This was good news!

"It was so great. It was like you knew just how to convince her!" Ivy was so excited that the words seemed to tumble out of her mouth. Happy nodded his head — it had all been part of the plan.

"Now we have to prove to her that we're

a good riding team, too. We'll only get one chance," Ivy continued. "But here's the best part. I get to ride you in my next lesson."

Ivy grinned and hugged Happy around the neck. Happy was glad that the plan had worked. But he was even more glad to see Ivy smiling again.

Later that day, Happy was back out in the field with his friends. He was still in a good mood, but something was worrying him. If Ivy rode him in her next lesson, she would not be riding Goldi. Happy felt bad. He didn't want to take Ivy away from Goldi.

Goldi had been a good friend to Happy. She had given him advice about being a school pony. She had told him stories about his mother. Happy knew he should tell Goldi about his lesson with Ivy. As Happy ate grass next to Goldi and Big Ben, he thought about what to say. But nothing seemed right.

After a while, Big Ben spoke up. "Prudence told me a funny story this morning," the show horse said in between bites. "It was about you, Happy. She said you didn't want to come in yesterday."

Happy swallowed. He had forgotten that Prudence had seen everything. She had watched him trot away from Diane again and again. He could not imagine how that had looked to the cat.

"Oh, that's right," Goldi said. "You were still in the field when we went inside." When she looked at Happy, she tilted her head to the side, and her long mane fluttered in the wind.

Happy sighed, trying to decide where to begin. "It's true. Roscoe and I came up with a plan," Happy explained. He told his friends

60

why he didn't come when Andrea had called. And why he had run away from Diane in the field. "I just wanted to show them that I think Ivy is special."

"Ivy *is* special," Goldi agreed. "And she is a good rider. I think it is time for her to move on to another pony. She has learned everything she can from me."

Happy took a deep breath. "I think she might ride me in her next lesson," Happy said.

"That sounds like a good match to me," Big Ben announced.

"Yes," Goldi said. "You will take good care of her. I'll miss her in lessons. She is very kind. But you two will be a good pair."

Happy kicked at the ground and looked away. What a relief! Goldi had said such nice things. "I'll do my best to keep her safe," he promised.

"Yes, you do that," Big Ben advised with a brisk nod of his head.

Goldi nodded, too. Then the three friends dropped their heads and happily buried their muzzles in the grass.

That evening, when Diane came to the pasture gate, Happy trotted toward her right away. He wanted her to know that he was still a good pony, and that he deserved to carry Ivy.

"Well, hello," Diane said.

As Diane clipped a lead rope on Happy's halter, Happy whinnied good night to his friends.

"Thanks for coming in right away, Happy," Diane said with a smile. She led him to the barn. "You're a smart pony, aren't you?"

Happy gave Diane a long look. What was she trying to say?

"I think you knew exactly what you were doing last night," Diane told Happy, running her hand through his silky black mane as they walked.

Happy was surprised. Did she really understand? Happy thought that Diane must be pretty smart, too.

"Well, your lesson with Ivy is tomorrow," Diane said as she opened his stall door. "Rest up, Happy. It will be a big day."

Happy walked right into his stall. Tomorrow! He could hardly believe it.

Diane closed the door and turned the bolt. "See you tomorrow, Happy!" she called. Then she went back outside to bring in the other horses.

Happy was so excited. He wished Roscoe were there, so he could tell his friend the good news. He looked around, but he did not see the mouse anywhere. He *did* see a scruffy orange cat sitting at the back of his stall, though. Prudence!

"Hello, Prudence," Happy said. Happy was in such a good mood, he didn't feel scared of her at all. "Did you hear the news?" he asked. "I'm going to carry Ivy in her lesson!"

"So it's true," Prudence said. She frowned, and her whiskers drooped down. "Diane is really letting Ivy ride you." The cat stood up and leaped to the top of the stall door. When she turned around, she was shaking her head. "And I always thought Diane was smart."

Chapter Nine

Not a Perfect Day

Happy tried not to let Prudence's comment upset him, but it did dampen his spirits. When he went to sleep, he was full of doubts about the big lesson.

The next day, he woke up and heard the rain. More bad news. He did not like to be ridden in the rain. He had wanted his first lesson with Ivy to be perfect.

But when Ivy arrived in the barn, she

acted like it was the most beautiful day ever. She greeted Happy with a bright smile, and she gave him a pat. Then she brushed him all over. His coat was shinier than ever. He didn't even mind when she picked his hooves.

By the time Ivy led Happy out of his stall, he was feeling much better about the rain and everything else. But Ivy did not turn Happy toward the outdoor arena. They were headed for the indoor ring. Happy had never been ridden there before.

Diane smiled as they entered the ring. "Well, Ivy, this is it. Your big chance!"

"Hi, Mom," Ivy said. "Hi, Prudence."

Diane was sitting on top of a big barrel in the center of the ring. Prudence was sitting on another barrel, right next to Diane. Prudence acted like she was washing her front paw, but Happy knew she was eyeing them.

Happy looked all around. The indoor ring looked much different than it did from his stall. It was a large, open room with soft dirt on the ground. The roof was very high. It looked like it was made of some kind of metal, and Happy could hear the *ping* as the rain hit the roof. It made him nervous, but he knew he needed to think about other, more important things.

"We can do this, Happy," Ivy said. Her voice sounded far more serious than it had back in Happy's stall.

Ivy led Happy over to the stair block and pulled herself into the saddle. Happy could not believe how light she was! Her legs did not reach as low as his other riders' legs. The stirrups only came halfway down his belly. As they started to walk around the ring, Happy noticed that Ivy held the reins just right — not too loose and not too tight.

"Prepare to trot," Diane announced.

"Okay, Happy," Ivy whispered. "Just remember, we need to listen to each other." Happy's ears flicked back as he took in Ivy's words.  "I trust you," she said, reaching far forward so she could scratch behind his ear.

"And trot," Diane instructed.

Ivy sat back in the saddle. Then she clicked with her tongue and gave Happy a tap with her heels. Happy knew just what Ivy had asked. He picked up a trot, pushing his legs forward in long strides.

"Looking good," called Diane.

"He feels great!" Ivy said. Happy could tell by the sound of Ivy's voice that she was smiling.

He put extra spring in his step. Things were going well. But when they reached the top of the ring, they had to go past the door. The inside ring had a huge door that rolled open to the outside. When it was open, it was big enough for several horses to walk through at the same time. It was closed now, but Happy could hear wind sweeping through the cracks. The wind made a high whistle, and Happy didn't like it at all. He didn't want to go near that door!

"Don't let him shy away from the door, Ivy," Diane advised. "Take him deep into the corners, so he has to trot right by it."

"Okay," Ivy said. Happy was already trying to turn away, but Ivy did what her mother said. With a strong pull on the reins, she guided him into the corner.

Happy's body tensed up as he got close. He could hear the whine of the wind. He closed his eyes. What a terrible sound! But Ivy gave him a squeeze with her legs, so he kept moving. The next thing Happy knew, they were already past the door. Thank goodness!

"Nice work, Ivy," Diane said. Out of the corner of his eye, Happy could see that she had a little smile on her face.

"Good boy, Happy," Ivy whispered. "That wasn't so bad, was it?"

Happy had to agree. He relaxed, and he let himself enjoy trotting again. He was amazed that Ivy sat so smoothly in the saddle. He knew she was there, but she didn't bounce or yank on the reins like other riders.

The next time Happy rounded the corner toward the door, Ivy held the reins steady. She gave him a little kick so he didn't slow down, and soon he had passed the door again.

"I knew you could do it," Ivy said.

Happy was feeling better and better about the lesson. He could ignore the *ping* of the rain on the roof. He could get past the gigantic door. After they trotted, Happy and Ivy cantered in both directions. When they came back to a walk, he was sure Diane had given them a nod of approval. Not even Prudence was scowling anymore.

"Okay, Ivy," Diane said. "You and Happy are looking good. How about you trot him up over this little fence."

A jump! Happy was so excited. He loved to jump, but he hadn't done it since Andrea had been riding him. None of the other kids had asked him to go over a fence during a lesson.

"Really?" Ivy asked.

"Yes, let's do it," Diane announced. "I think you two are ready. Just trot over the blue-and-white jump."

Happy remembered what Roscoe had told him. Ivy was new at jumping, so Happy would have to be especially good. Happy felt Ivy tighten the reins. She asked him to trot.

The fence was at the top part of the ring, just on the other side of the big door. Happy took a deep breath and started to trot. The blue-and-white jump came closer and closer. He rounded the corner before the door. They were only a few strides away when a loud crashing sound echoed through the indoor ring.

A mighty rumble of thunder rattled the barn walls, and Happy was filled with fear. *Bang!* Now every *ping* on the roof made Happy tremble. The wind shrieked through the cracks in the big door. Happy couldn't escape. He took off. He swerved right around the blue-and-white fence and ran as fast as he could. He had to get away from those sounds!

He pushed his legs faster and faster. He galloped around the outside of the ring, looking for somewhere to go. He couldn't think of anything except getting away. He had to run!

Happy forgot about the fence. He forgot about the lesson. He even forgot about Ivy.

Chapter Ten

Ivy and Happy

As Happy bolted around the ring, Ivy held on. He might have forgotten about her, but she had not forgotten about him. Eventually, Happy could hear her tiny voice over the pounding of his hooves.

"It's okay, Happy," Ivy said. She spoke in an even tone. "Don't worry, I'm still here." Happy's ears flickered back. He could barely hear her, but he wanted to know what she was saying.

"It's okay, Happy," Ivy said again. "I still trust you."

This time, Happy could just understand her words. *She still trusts me.* His legs continued to gallop, but he now could feel Ivy on his back. He felt her pull gently on the reins, and he told himself he could slow down. If he slowed down, Ivy would still be there. Everything would be fine.

Happy went from a gallop to a canter, a canter to a trot, and a trot to a walk. Ivy talked to him the whole time. "You're all right," she said.

Happy was breathing very hard, and his whole body was still tense. Ivy stroked his sweaty neck. Then, another roll of thunder rattled the barn. Happy shook with fear, but he did not start to run. He listened to Ivy.

"You're okay," she said again. "We'll be okay."

But then Happy realized that they wouldn't be okay. He had ruined everything. He had been too scared. He had bolted during their lesson. Now Diane would say they weren't a good team.

Just then, Diane let out a loud sigh. "Nice work, Ivy," she called. "You got him to listen to you. Now walk him around the ring a few times. He needs to catch his breath."

As Happy went around the ring with Ivy still on his back, he mumbled to himself. *Why did I let the thunder scare me? It just sounded so much louder than it ever did at Shoemaker Stables. The whole barn shook!* Happy understood why he had been scared, but that didn't solve his problem. *All I had to do was jump that little fence. I knew it was my*

only chance to prove I was good enough for Ivy. Now I've ruined it.

But Ivy did not sound upset. She still spoke to him in her kind voice, petting his neck.

"Okay, Ivy," Diane announced. "Let's try the jump again."

Happy lifted his head. *Really? Diane is going to let us try again?* Happy glanced over at Diane. Her face was serious. Prudence was looking at Diane, too. The cat was clearly shocked.

"Prepare to trot," Diane announced.

Ivy shortened her reins and nudged Happy with her heels. The pony stepped forward. When Ivy gave him another nudge, he picked up his pace.

"That's good, Happy," Ivy said. She guided Happy into the corner, and then turned him. Now he could see the blue-and-white fence. It was coming closer and closer. Happy pricked his ears forward. He passed the gigantic door. He could hear the wind whistle, but he could also hear Ivy click her tongue. She was encouraging him. Now he was just two strides away from the fence. He lifted his front legs, and his back legs pushed him over the jump. They were on the other side!

"Good job!" Diane called.

Ivy patted Happy again and again. "Good boy, Happy!" she said, her voice still sweet and soft.

"How about you come into the center of the ring?" Diane said.

Ivy turned Happy around, and they walked over to where Diane was sitting. Now Happy wasn't afraid of the gigantic door or the thunder, but he was afraid to hear what Diane would say.

"Well," Diane began, "you two looked great together until the storm really started. Then it was obvious that Happy is still young, and a lot of things are new to him."

"But he was scared," Ivy said.

Diane took a breath. "Yes, he was scared. And all ponies get scared from time to time," she agreed. "The important part is that he listened to you. And he didn't stop running just because you pulled on the reins. He stopped running because he trusts you." Diane paused. "Then he was willing to try the jump again. I think that's a very good sign."

"You mean . . . ?" Ivy asked.

Diane nodded. "I mean you can keep taking lessons on him, as long as you both continue to show that you can be a good team."

Happy couldn't believe it! Ivy wrapped her arms around his neck, and Happy felt safe and content. He now knew what Big Ben had been saying in the field that day. For a pony, there really is nothing better than having a rider who understands you.

Ivy walked Happy around the ring until he was nice and cool. Then she took him to his stall and brushed him from head to toe.

The whole time, she told him what a good pony he had been. Happy nuzzled her with his nose to tell her that she was a good rider. But he knew they were more than just a pony and rider. They were friends. Today, Ivy had taken care of Happy. And some days, it would be Happy who took care of Ivy.

When Ivy was done brushing Happy, she pulled two apples out of her backpack. "One for you, and one for me," she said. Ivy stood next to Happy while they ate, and when she was only halfway done, she gave him the rest of her apple. "I have to go home now, Happy. But I'll come and see you tomorrow." Then she kissed him on his nose and closed his stall door.

Happy stuck his head into the aisle and watched his friend go. After she had turned the corner, he heard a voice.

"Ahem."

Happy looked around to see Prudence sitting across the aisle from his stall.

"Hello, Happy," the cat said.

"Hello, Prudence." Happy's body went stiff. He was not comfortable when Prudence was around.

"I want to offer my apologies," Prudence said. "I was wrong about you. You might be young, but you are wise — wise  enough to know that Ivy will look out for you."

Happy was surprised.

"That thunder was loud," Prudence admitted. "You had every right to be scared. It even rattled an old barn cat like me. But you proved that you trust Ivy, and I can tell she trusts you." Prudence paused to scratch her ear with her back leg. Then she stretched her two front legs.

"You see," the cat continued, "I really like Ivy. She's still young, like you. So I look out for her. And I'll keep looking out for her. That's just what I do." Then Prudence stood up and started to strut away.

Happy finally found his voice. "Thank you, Prudence," he called. "And thank you for looking out for Ivy."

"Sure," the tabby said without looking back. "All in a day's work."

Happy sighed. It had been a busy day. There was so much to think about! As he turned around in his stall, he saw a welcome smile.

"Roscoe!" Happy was pleased to see him. The mouse was perched in the gap in the back wall of the stall, grinning widely.

"Hey, Happy," Roscoe said. "Did you have a good day at riding school?"

Happy laughed. "Yes, I did."

"So our plan really worked!" The mouse gave Happy a high five on the nose. "Why don'tcha tell me all about it?" Then Roscoe scampered across the floor and climbed up the side of the grain bucket. He sat on the edge and looked at Happy.

Happy smiled. It was nice to have good friends like Roscoe around. It was true that Happy was young and still had a lot to learn, but Happy now knew that was okay. He could count on his friends — Roscoe, Ivy, Goldi, Big Ben, and even Prudence — to be there to help. And Happy would always be willing to help them, too. Happy thought that being there for your friends was the best plan of all.

Glossary
The Gaits of a Pony

The word "gait" is used to explain a horse or pony's movements. The gait describes both how a pony moves, and how fast he moves. The four main gaits are the walk, trot, canter, and gallop. These gaits are in order from slowest to fastest.

In the **walk**, there are four beats, meaning each hoof hits the ground at a separate time.

The **trot** has two distinct beats. The trot can be bouncy, so riders often rise up and down out of the saddle to avoid hitting the pony's back. This up-and-down motion is called posting.

The **canter** is even faster than a trot. It has three beats. The canter starts with a back leg pushing the pony forward and has an obvious rocking motion.

The **gallop** is the fastest gait. It is a lot like the canter, but the pony moves at a faster speed and its hooves hit the ground one at a time, so the gallop has four beats. During the gallop, the rider should rise slightly out of the saddle while keeping the heels down. This allows the pony to move without straining its back.

Some breeds of ponies are born with the ability to move in additional gaits, and sometimes ponies can be trained to learn a different gait. But the walk, trot, canter, and gallop are the four most common.

About the Author

Kristin Earhart grew up in Worthington, Ohio, where she spent countless waking and sleeping hours dreaming about horses and ponies. She started riding lessons at eight, and her trainer really was named Diane. Kristin made a lot of good friends at Riverlea stables. In fact, Kristin's pony, Moochie, and her horse, Wendy, were two of the best friends a girl could ever have. She lives in Brooklyn, New York, with her husband and their son.